Nathan S. S. Beman

Our Civil War

the principles involved, its causes and cure, being a discourse delivered on

Thanksgiving day, Nov. 27, 1862

Nathan S. S. Beman

Our Civil War
the principles involved, its causes and cure, being a discourse delivered on Thanksgiving day, Nov. 27, 1862

ISBN/EAN: 9783337221188

Printed in Europe, USA, Canada, Australia, Japan

Cover: Foto ©Andreas Hilbeck / pixelio.de

More available books at **www.hansebooks.com**

Our Civil War:

THE PRINCIPLES INVOLVED,

ITS

CAUSES AND CURE,

BEING

A Discourse

DELIVERED ON THANKSGIVING DAY,

NOV. 27, 1862.

N. S. S. BEMAN.

TROY, N. Y.:

A. W. SCRIBNER & CO., PRINTERS, CANNON PLACE.

1863.

(

DISCOURSE.

—- •◆• —--

PSALM 83: 4.

" They have said, come and let us cut them off from being a Nation,—that the name of Israel may be no more in remembrance."

ISAIAH 8: 11-13.

" For the Lord spake thus to me with a strong hand, and instructed me, that I should not walk in the way of this people, saying, say ye not A confederacy, to all them to whom this people shall say A confederacy ; neither fear ye their fear, nor be afraid. Sanctify the Lord of hosts himself; and let him be your fear, and let him be your dread."

I shall make no apology to this audience, for occupying the present hour in giving you what is commonly called a political sermon. The crisis in our history imposes a duty upon all good citizens which the loyal in heart cannot well resist. And this duty rests with no less weight upon the minister at the altar, than upon any other member of the community. Indeed, the special oath of God is upon him, and he should be careful to maintain a good conscience before his fellow-countrymen and the world, as well as before high heaven. He has no right, in any circumstances, or under any pretext, to ignore, or repudiate, or shoulder aside, those obligations which bind him to the social structure of which he is an individual element, or a constituent part.

The popular prejudice which exists in our day and in our country, against an occasional discussion in the pulpit, and especially on a week day, of some great subject which relates to the policy of the government and the good of the people as a social body, is a problem which philosophy has not yet fully solved. The old prophets were in the habit of instructing, and even reproving, rulers, when occasion required,—and warning the people touching national measures; and no one thought it out of place. The preachers of the Revolution were among the most out-spoken and zealous patriots, and delivered sermons, not only on special occasions, but often on the Sabbath, exhorting the half-discouraged people to stand by their country, in the dark day of her calamities; and nobody complained, but the tories. The Southern clergymen, who, next to the politicians, have done more than any other men to kindle the fires of rebellion, and fan them into the intensest flame, have preached and published the most inflammatory discourses against our blessed Union; and their broad and unsparing denunciations have been advertised and read at the North, and praised by the disloyal among us ; and not a stain of evil has been detected in their pages, by such murmurers about *political preaching.*

And after all, who is it, that is most deeply grieved, by such discussions in the pulpit, in our day, and among us ? There may be, and no doubt *is*, here and there a good man—a truly pious man—who conscientiously thinks, that the pulpit should never admit any thing else than the naked law of God and the pure gospel of Jesus Christ—and that, too, in the most literal sense :— that the government of the country, and the civil and political rights of the people, should never be discussed or hinted at there, because the place is too holy for such themes. But the number to which I now refer, is very small. The great mass of those who shudder at political sermons as *profane*, are those who care not a fig for religion. They are too often men who are found in the precincts of the grog-shop, and breathe its pestiferous air, and derive their religious inspiration and zeal from its predominant and pervading element. And I may add, in our day, they are those whose loyalty is doubtful, and who might say, under such a sermon, as one said in behalf of his whole class or profession, under a discourse of the great preacher.—" Master, thus saying thou reproachest us also."

The two passages I have placed at the head of this discourse, as a sort of suggestive text, relate to two distinct historical events, but of the same political character. The passage from the 83d Psalm, written by a descendant of the celebrated singer and poet, Asoph, relates to a formidable conspiracy against the throne of David, in the reign of Jehoshaphat King of Judah. Israel rebelled, and Judah was loyal. The traitors formed a motley crew, composed of Apostate Hebrews, and associated Heathen, and half-breeds. They were crafty in counsel and tumultuous in their vain boastings. They said, "Come, and let us cut them off from being a nation,—that the name of Israel may be no more in remembrance." Certain political and moral reformations inaugurated by Jehoshaphat, had contributed to stir up and intensify this special enmity at that time. These " confederates " could not bear that such a nation should exist and prosper, or its memorial leave a vestige on the page of history. They had become desperate.

The passage from Isaiah relates to a combination of the apostate house of Israel with certain foreign powers, against the Kingdom of Judah, and the house of David. It was a rebellion against a government formed and established by God himself,—and occurred in the days of Sennacherib, some 150 years subsequent to the insurrection of "the confederates" already referred to. It is strongly intimated in this divine record, that there was a large party in Judah who sympathized with the enemies of the government, through fear or some other unworthy motive; but the prophet was warned against fellowship with such. "For the Lord spake thus to me with a strong hand, and instructed me, that I should not walk in the way of this people, saying, say ye not A confederacy to all them to whom this people shall say A confederacy; neither fear ye their fear nor be afraid. Sanctify the Lord of hosts himself; and let him be your fear, and let him be your dread." It is much better, and much safer to fear God, than the rebels. They are antagonistic powers, and God is stronger than men.

There is a voice uttered in the context, which seems to have been spoken prophetically for the men of our day, both here upon our own soil and abroad among foreign nations. "Associate yourselves, O ye people, and ye shall be broken in pieces; and give ear, all ye of far countries : gird yourselves, and ye shall be broken in pieces ; gird yourselves, and ye shall be broken in pieces. Take counsel together, and it shall come to naught;

speak the word, and it shall not stand, for God is with us."

It is worthy of note, that the term "Confederacy," now in political and popular use, occurs but three times in the Scriptures—twice in my text from Isaiah and once in Obadiah—and always in a bad and odious sense. It is only another name for a wicked *conspiracy* against a legitimate and heaven-established government. "Confederate," which stands in the context of the passage from the Psalms, likewise is used but three times in the Bible, once in a good sense, for powers bound in treaty stipulations for mutual defence, and twice, for base *conspirators* against the divine institution of civil government. The Southern rebels seem to have been divinely directed, *in one thing*,—in selecting a descriptive name for themselves and their government. They are "Confederates," or *conspirators*, and their government a "Confederacy," or *conspiracy!* We may say of this wonderful adaptedness of names to the things indicated, as the magicians once said to Pharaoh,—"This is the finger of God." He has secretly and mysteriously led them to write unwittingly their own history, and delineate graphically their own character. There is a directing providence in the affairs of men; and God lives in human history. And he will live there, through the ages. "There is a Divinity that shapes our ends, rough hugh them as we will."

The picture of our country, at this day, in contrast with what we have seen it from our earliest years, is truly affecting. If it were not for sterner duties which urge us to more manly deeds, we might well sit down here, and weep patriot tears over the changes which have passed, and are passing around us. A brilliant sky was once over our heads, but the stars by night are now dimmed, and the sun by day is suffering a disastrous eclipse. A preternatural midnight, in the early evening, has settled down upon all that just now smiled in beauty and loveliness around us. And the picture has warm blood-drops upon it. Death breathed upon it, and it withered,—touched it with his finger, and defaced and marred it. The grave-digger, with his spade on his shoulder, is stealing through the mysterious darkness, having opened, and then filled, two hundred thousand graves with friends and foes—with murdered citizens and dead traitors. With all our manhood we might well weep like women, over these desolations which have fallen upon our country. The silent sleepers beneath our feet, have here and there a memento to tell us who they are, but most of them lie in solitary, or in promiscuous, or mingled oblivion— " alike unknowing and unknown."

2

The *treasures* wasted in this national conflict, are untold. One thousand million, at least, have gone down into the deep ocean, to come up no more. It might occur to your minds as a fact, affording some relief, that nearly one half of this sum was a fictitious rebel currency—worth nothing at the beginning, and no better now, and not likely to improve in time to come. And yet the loss has fallen on *somebody*. Material good has been sacrificed, and the means of life and happiness annihilated. They are gone for ever.

And look at this beautiful earth which God has spread beneath our feet,—smiling in youthful promise, and teeming with uncounted wealth. Yesterday, it was so.—to-day, how marred, and scorched, and cursed. Here fields are unreaped and harvests trodden down,—and there, of equal native fertility, they lie uncultivated and fallow. Fine old forests are felled to the earth to obstruct the march of invading armies, and all is martial pomp and array. Tents whiten the hill tops and the valleys, batteries are planted every where, cities and towns are surrounded with intrenchments and walled by strong fortifications, and fields that once welcomed the plow-share with a smiling promise, become battle grounds where death rules the hour! The clash of arms and the thunder of artillery rend the air, the death struggle

ensues, strong men are stricken down, and the
earth smokes, and the rivers are purpled with
human blood. Some of the fairest portions of our
land have become a desolation. But the half has
not been told you. I would not attempt to tell
you. My powers could not compass the magni-
tude of the evils, or my tongue utter a tithe of
their horrors.

But who, or what, has done all this? What
fiend, exiled from light and heaven, has visited us,
and left his cloven foot-prints upon the fairest land
that ever smiled in the face of the opening skies?
Surely a great foe has been here, and done this
fearful deed. It is a DEVIL *baptized* "SECESSION."
He has done all this, and he intends to do more.
This embodiment of all political evils, claims the
right of breaking up the government formed by
our fathers, by going out of the Union by States.
If one man should do such a deed, he would be
hanged If a voluntary combination of individuals, should attempt the same, a like fate would
overtake them. But if a *State* does the foul deed,
the panoply of "State Rights" is an ample protection in the opinion of some. Mr. Buchanan stood
amazed, and looked at this fiend, till his heart,
which was never known to have any other fiber
in it, than that of *ambition*, actually began to soften,
and he almost fell in love with it. It seemed all

but "an angel of light,"—and it became more beautiful, the longer he gazed. It was so near faultless, that it would be unconstitutional and unkind to resort to the use of any "coercion" in dealing with it. Treason must be *coaxed*, and not *coerced*, out of its villiany. This tame policy has well nigh made ship-wreck of this republic. It would have done it, if God had not brought in new agencies to the rescue. And some men feel quite grieved and angry that the old party in power had not continued to direct the destinies of the nation, till the ruin was fully consummated, and our fate sealed beyond redemption.

The right of " secession," either by individuals, or combinations of men, or organized State authorities—is a bald absurdity. In speaking to sensible men, it would be a waste of time and words to construct a grave and formal argument to prove this fact. Admit the principle and claims of secession, and you blot out all law. Its soul, or essence, which is *penalty*, is annihilated ; the letter is nailed to the gibbet ; and if it retains the semblance of an organic existence, it is a dead letter. " It is henceforth good for nothing, but to be cast out, and trodden under foot of men." Compacts and Constitutions, ratified with solemn deliberation, and consecrated with prayer, and cemented with pure, patriot blood, become foot-balls for wiley demagogues, and are impelled to and fro, as mere playthings. We have seen so much of this in our day, that we have come to an utter loathing of such political hypocrisy. The men who framed and adopted our Constitution were honest men; and they took it for granted, that their descendants would possess both the intelligence and integrity to carry out its letter and spirit. But they placed, I fear, too high an estimate upon both. The modern doctrine of "States' Rights"—investing these rights with supremacy—and arming them with a power to override the general government, destroys at once the very existence of a nation. The Union is a compact at will. Any member can retire at his option : and if *one* may, *all* may, and the powers of the government, and solemn stipulations, and foreign alliances, and the signs and symbols which indicate an organic nationality, are swept away at a blow. This is the political heresy which has infatuated some otherwise sane minds, and endangered our God-given institutions, and cursed our once blessed land. This imp of darkness has brought forth those " *wayward sisters*," and then educated them thoroughly in her own school, whose charms have so smitten some of our modern politicians, that they long to go down to Richmond, and have a fraternal interview, and then " bid them depart in peace." The man who holds the doctrine, and practices upon it—that any State may, at her option, retire from the compact—ratified by the Constitution, and leave the Union a shattered fragment—*is a traitor and a rebel*; and *he* is no less a traitor and a rebel, who denies this doctrine of state rights, and would, at the same time, suffer any member of the compact to retire from its position without the use of coercion and force to prevent it. The united powers of government and loyalty are pledged to prevent such a movement. That government which does not call into requisition all the material and means which heaven and earth may furnish to accomplish this end, deserves to be rent in atoms; and that professed loyalty which does not cordially unite in this work, and cry amen to every inch of its progress, and is not prepared to sing paeons of glory over its final triumph, is downright hypocrisy. It is empty profession, and nothing else.

The Author of that doctrine which paved the way to this rebellion, has damaged this government more than any other man who has ever enjoyed in a preeminent degree, its honors and emoluments. John C. Calhoun was a man by himself. He stood alone. He was the inventor of the *metaphysics of Politics*,—a cool and subtle reasoner, and his conclusions logical, if his postulates had not often been too bold and extravagant to be true, and sometimes so numerous as to shake our confidence in the strength of his argument. Admit his premises, and his inference follows. Many have adopted the inference without examining the premises with sufficient acumen to discover that they are assumed truths—without any reasons—which amount, as the logicians say, to "a begging of the question." He had but one idol, chattel slavery—and this he worshiped with all the devotion and tenacity of a native-born pagan. Iron man, as he was, he bent the knee to this power, and to this alone, and his youthful admirers, over whom he had great influence, bowed in company with him, and the clergy of the South, and especially the Old School Presbyterian brethren, came to the Jubilee; and Diana of the Ephesians was never hailed with louder acclamations, than, *this great* god of cotton : and now and then has been heard a distinct and loud and joyous response from the working men—the democratic masses, of the North.

The latter half of Mr. Calhoun's life was devoted to one grand purpose. For this every thing else must stand aside. Every opposing agency must bend or break. This object was, the extension and perpetuation of slavery. Whatever other interest may suffer, "this institution must be honored." This language was once uttered by himself. His genius and tact gave us Texas; and his doctrines finally broke up the "Missouri Compromise," and inaugurated the bloody scenes of Kansas. Without slavery we should never have had a Calhoun, as position and circumstances finally developed him; and without both—Calhoun and slavery—we should never have been visited by this afflictive civil war. Originally a radical democrat of the Jeffersonian school, he taxed all his talents and all his logic to reconcile his former sentiments with his new political and social theories. "The Declaration of Independence" which stared him in the face, he disposed of by a short process. Once—when I first knew him, it was the inspiration of his loftiest eloquence; now it was a work of the *imagination*, and utterly false in its positions and principles, or at least only poetically true. As to *the unalienable rights of man*—" life, liberty, and the pursuit of happiness," they must be interpreted with proper restrictions—first settling the question, that the black man is a mere outsider of the human race. Such a being was *created* for bondage, and not for freedom. God made him for this very purpose, and it would be *profane* to mar the workmanship of Almighty God. As Mr. Calhoun's heart was not all iron, he defended this divine arrangement on the ground of benevolence,—that servitude was the happiest possible condition for the colored race, and that some must be SLAVES, or none could be truly free. This is now the prevailing Southern doctrine, that slavery must exist in order to give the highest zest to freedom, and, at the same time, insure its permanency and triumph. And as Mr. Calhoun, was, by an early Presbyterian education, a believer in the divine purposes, he cherished the pious hope, that American *man-stealing* might not only bring many of these poor heathen across the Atlantic to this good land, but, after having given them some of the foretastes of heaven, in the earthly Paradise of Slavery, might carry them safely over Jordan to the better land of Canaan above.

The contest in which we are now engaged, is one of the most eventful that human passion has ever stirred up, or human arms, fiercely waged on earth. The democratic principle of self-government, is now on trial. Crowned brows, and starred shoulders, and mitered heads—the holy alliance of tyranny—are empanneled in the jury-box, and the world is now all attention to the arguments of cannon and musketry, in open court, and waiting anxiously for the verdict. Freedom, or oppression, will be jubilant at its rendering. Our experiment of self-government, has been tried under more auspicious circumstances, than any ·

3

previous one, since the world began. Our fathers had intelligence and virtue,—they formed a good constitution—not perfect, nothing human is,—they were firmly united together by the strong bonds which a death-struggle with a foreign foe, had created,—and God had given us a magnificent soil on which to plant our institutions, and begin our novel work. If this fails, where shall the attempt be made again,—and who shall commence it? If this star of hope to the nations, be extinguished, will the hand of God that once lighted it up for us—ever re-kindle it, in the darkened heavens? I tremble as I attempt to peer into the thick clouds which hang over the future. God alone can comprehend the great results. We may, however anticipate some of them with a probability which may not be likely to mislead us.

And among these we cannot fail to see, that, if the rebels prevail, and our Union is shattered, and our government broken up, the arm of the despot will be greatly strengthened by these calamities. That arm will be as heavy and rigid as iron. The cry has already been lifted up all over Europe, that *the democratic principle has been tried, and found wanting.* Man cannot govern himself. Combinations of men cannot govern themselves. Free institutions formed by the people for their own government, cannot stand. And the final effect of all this will be, "the divine right of kings" will strike its roots more deeply in every soil, and "human rights" will be more wantonly disregarded by all hereditary powers. It would be argument enough to point the slow-moving finger of scorn at the fragments of our republic, as they float down the stream of national ruin, and say, "There learn the end of all free institutions!" This has been said already—prematurely, I believe,—and tyrants have "grinned a ghastly smile," as they have said it.

And this is not all. If secession should prevail in any degree—either according to its own large expectations. or in a more limited sense, a great nation, which was fast coming up to take her seat by the side of the most powerful of the earth—is ruined. Her name which has waved triumphantly upon a Banner more beautiful than any other that floats o'er the land—or gleams on the sea, is blotted out. A star gone—and the CONSTELLATION is marred and dimmed. This hemisphere grows dark, and prophesies of dissolution. The long future which we have anticipated with so much hope *in God*, and so much hope *for man*, is covered with a dark, thick pall that no eye can penetrate. If imagination might speak, she would whisper, "Death lies beneath that portentious symbol." One State out of the Union by permission of the government, and another follows, and another, till the once seamless garment is rent in twain. Disintegration once begun, the process may never be stayed in its course, till the United States may be known only in history and chanted only in song. This is secession made perfect.

The influence of this country upon all the institutions of the old world, for the last twenty-five years, has been such as to reflect credit upon ourselves, and to create alarm in many other quarters. While there has been too much self-gratulation on our part, yet there is no merit in voluntary or affected ignorance on this subject. All the movements in behalf of freedom and the rights of man, in European governments, had their birth-place and education in the United States. The pagan world has felt the power of our free christianity; and many converts on the other side of the glode, having been cheered by our light, now join with us in prayer to God, that this light may never be dimmed, or extinguished. The Foreign Missionaries tell us, that the native christians take a deep interest in this our present national crisis. Should our government be prostrated and our country trodden under foot of rebels, there is not an interest of benevolence on our globe but would feel the shock, and be retarded. The missionary abroad would find his heart depressed and his hands weakened, and the great pagan world would pass into a super-added and deeper gloom. The dawn of the millenium would seem to recede again into its ancient midnight.

The statesmen and diplomatists of Europe, have become more and more alarmed at our influence upon their people; and they seem to feel, at least, a momentary relief from their fears since the traitors have uncaped their volcano among us. Nations whose civilization and progress should have inspired the deepest sympathy for us, and whose record in favor of humanity is before the world, have evidently begun to glory in our downfall, and to turn a cold shoulder to us in the hour of our trial. The feeling expressed has been this : 'Come, and let us cut them off from being a nation,—that their name may be no more in remembrance.' This clamor about freedom and the rights of man and human progress, is not to our taste, and we cannot endure it. The United States are becoming a dangerous rival, and with their growing power and wealth, the principles of their government will commend themselves more and more to men of thought and philanthrophy the world over. "Come, and let us cut them off from being a nation." 'This is our only sure protection.'

This train of thought has been indulged by many a Trans-Atlantic Statesman. The presence of such a nation as ours—free, active, self-governed, progressive—is fatal to the whole world of tyrants. We need not wonder, that the wiley Frenchman—USURPER as he is—should take an attitude against us,—or his half-starved and unstable millions should sympathize with him. But *England!* Who would have expected such a voice from England? And yet we have heard it. The throne and the people of that kingdom who generally stand together, are with us, in their " heart of hearts," in this fearful struggle for life,—but the *aristocracy*—proverbial for their hauteur and their contempt for the progress of the masses, and their ecclesiastical appendage—the established church of like taste and proclivities—are decidedly with the rebels. Their *heart* is there—because they have a like heart with them. Two that are agreed naturally walk together. There is an air of nobility in slave-holding. It gives leisure—gives luxury—gives power over man—and gives wealth and refinement. It secures a sort of hereditary distinction,—an entailed nobility. Take it all in all—there is a charming odor about it,—a delightful flavor. In one word slavery is *beautiful.* And, then, the slaves toil not less for Manchester, than for Richmond. And they both reap a rich harvest from fields cultivated by slave-labor. While the operatives of the one city are kept from starving, the citizens of the other " are clothed in scarlet and fine linen and fare sumptuously every day." We see then that the aristocracy and clergy of England and the Southern Confederacy are bound together by a strong material and social tie. And we need not wonder at what is said in high places in Great Britain. There is no mystery in these utterances. To a philosophical mind, they expound themselves. Take a few of them as samples, on this occasion.

England has declared ' that *slavery* has nothing to do with this rebellion and this civil war,—that freedom would rather lose than gain with the triumph of the North,—that the South and the North were already two nations.' Such utterances are a compound of stupidity and perverseness,—and, in this country, can only provoke a smile or a sneer. Earl Russell summed up the whole matter by saying, " that the contest was, on the part of the North, for supremacy, on the South, for independence." Mr. Gladstone echoes this most profound sentiment of the noble Earl. It was discovered, as long ago as the days of Elihu, that " Great men are not always wise."

Lord Brougham describes this war as the " frantic rage of a whole people, filled with a thirst for vengeance, only to be slaked by each other's slaughter." Poor old lord! His hatred of democracy, or a popular government, has swallowed up and annihilated his once vigorous anti-slavery zeal,—and he sees nothing in the struggles of this civil war, 'but the *visions of free-trade*, and the fury of such a mob as that which demanded of Pontius Pilot the crucifixion of Jesus Christ.' Most of the LITERARY AND RELIGIOUS PERIODICALS of Great Britain, are in sympathy with the South against the North. THE LONDON REVIEW, published by the Wesleyans, is the only respectable exception. Dr. Campbell of the *Standard*, assures us that "no power on earth can alter his views." Probably not, for he is an obstinate Scotchman. "A wise man changes his opinion sometimes, a fool never."

At a meeting of the Guildford Agricultural Association, the Rev. G. Portal, Rector of Aldbury, delivered his cruel soul as follows:—

"If war should unhappily arise between the two countries, he hoped there would be no more of that maudlin sentimentality, of which we had heard so much, about the Americans being our blood relations, and that a war with them would be as bad as civil war at home. It was all nonsense. America separated from us a century ago, and since then her population had been recruited from every country of the world. In New York there were more than 200,000 Germans, and those who know what 'points' it took to establish similarity of *breed* must be aware what sort of similarity existed between us and that country. He was very much of the opinion of the writer who said, that a Yankee was as great a parody upon an Englishman, as a monkey was upon the human race."

This savage speech was made about the time of the affair of the Trent. It was a dark—dark day in English intellect. A general lunacy broke loose among the people, at that period. In a time of general national dementation, it is truly cheering to meet with such names as these :— Arthur, the noble Wesleyan,—Bright, the pure-minded and honest Quaker,—and Mill, the acute political economist. They have uttered words of encouragement when most needed by us,—and they have uttered words of fearful warning which will come up in the reminiscences of others,—of a selfish and infatuated nation, when the day of retribution shall arrive. Whether our Rector of Aldbury, spoke under the influence of the prevailing national lunacy, I will not undertake to pronounce. The law of nature exempts some men from mental derangement. He that is born a fool, can never become a maniac.

4

England is the living, and unexpounded, Riddle, of our world. Without exhausting the subject, DeTocqueville has made a few happy hits which very naturally occur to the mind in connection with these expressions of British opinion on our civil war. "In the eyes of an Englishman," says this shrewd and philosophical writer, "a cause is just, if it be the interest of England that it should succeed. A man or a government that is useful to England has every kind of merit, and one that does England harm, every sort of fault." And again, It is "the conviction of all nations, that England considers them only with reference to her own greatness, that she never notices what passes among foreigners, what they think, feel, suffer, or do—but with relation to the use which England can make of their actions, their sufferings, their feelings, and their thoughts: and that when she seems most to care for them, she really cares only for herself." If this is not a life-like portrait of England, drawn by a master's hand,—then, whose portrait is it? These few graphic phrases, applied by an analytic mind, will place England before the world in revelations that will appear little less than miraculous. Here is a key more infallible than that of St. Peter, which will unlock most of the political mysteries of the sea-girt isle in 1861-2,—and it may be some others yet to come.

Here is the Trent affair, with all the jesuitical twistings and turnings, in broad day light, and at the expense of precedents, professions, and practice, on the part of England. They have had to swallow a whole volume of their naval history, before they could assume the ground they have taken. It is not the thing done, but the persons doing it and the time in which the act was performed. Here you see Palmerston and Russell, and Gladstone giving opinions and making declarations, respecting our country, which belie all the facts of current history, and the blunders of which would disgrace a common school-boy—and for a purpose which is branded upon their very face—in order to exalt England and pull down a growing rival. Here is a nation just escaped from a fearful civil war, in which they had our sympathies, turning the current of these good wishes, and their material aid too, so far as they can do it and keep up a certain *anamalous something*, which they call "*a strict neutrality,*" in favor of a *slave-holding rebellion*, prompted only by ambition and the love of power. England has done this in the very face of all her former declarations and acts against human bondage,—thus blotting with ineffaceable stains the fairest page of her history. Mark me, though not a prophet, nor the son of a prophet,—an earthly retribution is before that nation.

Sad mistakes in the prosecution of this war, on our part, have entailed upon us most disastrous and disgraceful failures. It should have been ended long ago. It might have been. It is a burning shame to the strong, loyal North—with her twenty millions, and her large resources of every kind, that it has not been done. I know it is easy to criticise, and find fault, and condemn. The genius of human nature excels in this department of execution: and yet, to a generous mind, it is by no means a coveted task. But the fact cannot be disguised, that there has been blame somewhere. Two great mistakes may embrace the sum and substance of the whole. These are generic. We have underrated the work to be done, and we have mistaken and misapplied the means in order to effect it.

The project of bringing back ten revolted States to their allegiance, and of pacifying five more in strong sympathy with them in social habits and domestic institutions, may be pronounced a great undertaking. It was once thought that many of the Southern people were truly loyal and a little assistance from the government, and the influence of a benign central power, would bring State after State, at the end of a short but bitter experience

of its erratic course, into its political orbit again.
But one problem has been fully solved. There is
no loyalty, *per se*, where the love of slavery is
deeply rooted in the heart. And this is as true in
one latitude as another. There is not one man in
a hundred among the border-state loyalists, whose
professed faith to the government is not based on
the safety of *negro property*. The Constitution
and oaths of allegiance, are dust in the balance
against the slave. One negro will turn the head,
and alienate the heart of any conditional loyal-
ist or patriot. His phrensy often rises so high,
when this interest is at stake—dearer than government, or country, or all else that is attractive, that
his full soul might well exclaim, in a parody on
the eloquent language of Patrick Henry—" Give
me my *negro*, or give me death." There are
some noble and disinterested exceptions to these
remarks.

And, then, few men could have anticipated the
strong sympathies and the material aid the insur-
rectionists against the best of governments, would
have received from England and France. They
have made a record for themselves which—to the
reproach of their civilization, will cling to their
name in after ages. I speak not of overt acts of
government, but of the spirit almost every where
cherished,—the *animus* pervading their speeches

and publications,—their *wishes*, intended to be kept secret, and yet but half concealed, and which crop out in their every day and minor acts. Any one can see that both of these nations long to do toward our government what, as yet, they have not dared to perpetrate in the broad day light of a christian world, and against the moral convictions of the nineteenth century. It would be an act which in the judgment of that world, and in such an age, *would insure universal reprobation for them.*

And few men who have not long and deeply studied our own national character, when either money, or partizan politics are concerned, could have believed that the free North would have done as much as England and France, to keep alive the fires of this rebellion. But so it is. Money is a great god to those who bow down and worship it; and there are politicians who never sleep except upon their arms ; and, when out of office, ever lie in ambush ready to spring upon their foe, like a tiger from his lair, in the moment when they least expect it. Had it not been for this lovely and loving fraternity—England, France, and Northern sympathisers with Southern villiany—quelling this rebellion would have been an easy work, and a short work. The traitors would have utterly failed for the want of bread and the munitions of war. The staff of life would have been broken, and the sinews of war cut and stranded. Here, then, in our circumstances, was a fearful work to be accomplished: much more so than our government supposed,—than any one living ever supposed.

The means to be employed, and the mode of applying them, would naturally take form and complexion from our estimate of the work to be achieved. The loving policy has been the order of the day. The truly energetic has never yet been in the ascendant. Nothing is ready when it is wanted. From the beginning the government has seemed to aim at conquering this rebellion without much bloody warfare. Stripes of kindness were to do the deed. Who initiated this policy—humane upon the face of it, but cruel and wasting in the bitter end—I know not. Some say President Lincoln is its author:—and he would naturally be under a strong temptation to adopt it, in order to conciliate the border-state men, who, as a class, I fear, have often done us more hurt than good. Some say Lieut. Gen. Scott, who was Commander-in-Chief of our armies, and to whom Old Virginia was ever dear as the apple of his eye, and seemed in his vision the very gem of perfectness. Or was it Gen. McClellan, the pupil of our venerable Chieftain ! or the heads of Department

—the constitutional advisers of the Executive!—
or all of these officials in joint counsel! I am impelled to ask these questions, but I cannot answer
them. Ten thousand loyal, and disappointed
citizens have asked the same. But it was a great
mistake whoever did it. They reckoned without
their host. They did not seem to know what stuff
Southern men are made of,—nor the long and
deadly purpose they have cherished to pull down
the pillars of this government, and shatter the
whole fabric into atoms, if they themselves should
finally be buried beneath its ruins. Leviathan is
not thus tamed. Love-tokens will not win him.
Hence we have been amused, as so many children,
with the tale of the speedy and pacific manner in
which this little Southern spree was to be closed
up. A strong cordon was to be thrown around
the revolted States, or most of them, and that to
intimidate, and not destroy; and then the bands
of love were to be drawn closer and closer, till
they sweetly returned into the Union without
hardly knowing how it was, and some of them
without even knowing they had ever been out
of it.

But this silken band is not entwined around the
rebels yet. We have always been about to do
something. But we have not done it. We have
had boast and bluster enough to satisfy any modest

man. Six months ago our grand army was about to press the whole insurgent foe "to the wall,"—but "the wall" has not been reached yet. At a later date, the audacious rebels came into Maryland to steal and pillage, and after dealing some sound blows upon them, we were told that "the enemy would soon be annihilated, and never re-cross the Potomac." They went back without obstruction, and are as well prepared for resistance to-day, as at any former period. It is to be hoped that the new military programme, under the control of another leader, and under better auspices, will effect something worthy of record. The loyal national heart beats with strong pulsations for that something.

In the prosecution of this war, "hope deferred, hath made the heart sick." Early last Spring the Mississippi river was to be opened from its head waters to the ocean; and all the sea ports from New Orleans to the mouth of the Potomac, were to be shortly ours, and a legitimate commerce again established with all the world, under the OLD "STARS AND STRIPES." I need not tell you how far we have succeeded, and where we have failed. Savannah is well fortified, and bids defiance to our beleaguering forces; and *Charleston*, that *old nest* of serpents, where rebellion was hatched and brooded, remains *statu quo*—poor, yet proud—

5

determined to resist to the last, and if the final hour must come, then her sons will commit this old Jezebel to a bondfire kindled by their own hands. This would be a merited fate. And then it should be plowed, as Zion of old was, and some divinely commissioned hand should sow it with salt, in token of its perpetual desolation. And thus the curse of heaven would rest upon the mother of rebels.

I have spoken of delays and reverses, and surely we have had enough to fill the cup of our national humiliation to the brim, and nearly enough to satisfy the malice of our bitterest foe. But God's hand is in these disappointments. They have not come causeless upon us, nor without his purpose and direction. We have not been sufficiently chastized as a nation. Our complicity with the great sin of the republic—*oppression*—has been sorely visited upon us, but I fear not yet to our humiliation and repentance. But our Father has taken his chastizing rod, and he will never lay it down till we are scourged out of many a national sin,—and, I believe, out of slavery among others. If we need more stripes, he will lay them on; and where the scene will end, and when, it is not given to mortal man to predict. God alone knows.

That we are not yet right, as a people, on the subject of chattel slavery, notwithstanding the vials of wrath it has poured out upon us, in this rebellion, is manifest from the enmity stirred up by the President's Proclamation in certain quarters. I mean his JUBILEE *proclamation.* I have often wished I could fully comprehend certain stereotyped phrases in vogue among editors and politicians in our day. Much is said of maintaining *the Constitution as it was.* This seems to be a plausible way of intimating, that whatever other interest may fail, or go uncared for, we must be sure and see that slaveholders are protected in their claims upon their chattels. But look upon this position for a moment. Would these men affirm, and have us believe, that the Constitution obliges us to return fugitive slaves to masters who are endeavoring to rend the government into fragments, and who employ these very slaves, when returned, to aid in this work of ruin? The guaranties of the Constitution were not made for such circumstances: and with the change of circumstances, the obligation ceases. Look at it as you will, and absurdity is branded upon its forehead. South Carolina says she is out of the Union, and will never return. The government may annihilate her, but can never bring her back. In this attitude, what relief can the Constitution bring her—either in the rendition, or the protection, of slaves! Let some Northern man tell us what he means by applying the Constitution as it was, or is, to this case. Or deny the claim, if you please, of South Carolina, and say she is not out of the Union; and, therefore, the government should fulfill all the stipulations of the old compact. Is this right secured to rebels who deny all obligation on their part, and who are armed to the teeth, to annihilate every legitimate power and interest of the government! This would certainly be an unusual stretch of political benevolence, that any government should feel itself bound to protect— and should feel disposed to protect, all the rights of insurgents and traitors in the same manner that she protects the rights of peaceful and loyal citizens. One might dream, that the fabled age of gold had visited our politicians. Or is it a softer age—the age of pewter in government, that has come upon us! And are these politicians to be known as pewter heads!

It should be remembered, in this connection, that a government involved in war, foreign or domestic, has certain prerogatives pertaining to that condition of things. Has any statesman ever denied to the war-power an inherent element that can reach *slavery*, or any other institution, which has a material bearing upon the issue of the conflict, and the government of which—either its protection or annihilation—may shorten the road to its peaceful end? I should like to hear such a denial from any man who has studied the laws of nations, or the laws of war. Till I hear the position taken by John Quincy Adams in the American Congress, challenged, or denied, by some authority, equally reputable, I am willing to rest upon that. "I lay this down," says this profound statesman, "as the law of nations. I say that military authority takes, for the time, the place of all municipal institutions, *and slavery among the rest*; and that, under that state of things, so far from its being true, that the states where slavery exists have the exclusive management of the subject, *not only the President of the United States, but the commander of the army has power to order the universal emancipation of the slaves.*"

This is the Constitution, as it was—is now—and, I hope, ever shall be, world without end. Its ordinary provisions are made for times of peace, —that is for ordinary times. But it has, as every human instrument should have, and must have, its *specialties*, which adapt it to times of *war*—foreign and domestic—and any other times that may occur. We need a Constitution, which, in its provisions and its interpretations, will afford us protection against an enemy from abroad and traitors at home. And such a Constitution we have ; and we may thank God that it has fallen into the hands of interpreters who will apply its every peace-power and war-power, so far as may be necessary, till this wicked rebellion is ground to powder. And it is a significant fact, that in the multitude of electioneering speeches with which we have been favored of late, filled with broad insinuations, that the constitution is in danger of being trodden under foot,—no man who has any reputation to hazard, has dared to deny, that the war-power gives the government of the United States the entire control over the institution of *slavery.* The doctrine stated and maintained on the floor of Congress, by ex-President Adams, has not been controverted, as far as I recollect, by any of our distinguished speakers, not even by our own New York orator, who has, at different times, said much about the *Constitution* and SLAVERY, and many other things, and who has richly earned for himself the SOBRIQUET—not of " *The Great Unknown,*" but of "THE GREAT UNRELIABLE." We have had insinuations and innuendoes enough about the Constitution, and its stipulations and violations,—but the man has not yet been found, who carries brass enough to say openly and frankly, that *the government of the United States is bound to return fugitive slaves to* REBELS, *or to pro-*

tect the claims of this institution in behalf of those who have renounced their allegiance, and who make war upon the Union. If there is such a man, I should like to see him.

I have perhaps said enough of the war policy by which our national movements have too generally been characterized. There was a time when men could have been had in any numbers, and this insurrection might have received its *quietus* in a few months. But the government had men enough, and refused more. Now the fervor has abated, and enlistments have lost their charm. If any more troops are called for, they must be procured by conscription. Northern patriotism, which I have always thought had a strong admixture of sudden passion and cool, calculating hypocrisy in it, if it has not expired, has burned down to a feeble flame, under various influences. Sympathy with the cause of the rebels, has become bold and outspoken,—politics have intervened to inspire the South with their old and long cherished hopes of democratic aid,—and our utter failure of giving to the country and the world some masterly warlike demonstration which should inspire the nations with the *facts of our actual power as it really exists*, may invite France to undertake the dictation of terms to our government. If such intervention should take place, my apprehension is that England will easily find some plausible reason for joining in this work of pure *benevolence*. The world knows, and Heaven knows, how these nations have always shuddered at the thought of shedding human blood. May God defend us, for vain is the help of man, and especially if we fall into the hands of such advisers: "Whose mouth speaketh vanity, and their right hand is a right hand of falsehood."

A more perfect contrast has rarely been presented to the human eye or mind, than by the two belligerent parties, in this country, arrayed against each other to-day. And this contrast you may trace in the aggregate and the minutiae—in the broad outline, and in the more delicate filling up. I speak not now of the decently uniformed, warmly clad, well shod, sumptuously fed army on the one side, and the butternut colored, fantastically attired, bare-footed, half-starved, motley crew on the other. There are many exceptions, I should say to this picture, on both sides. But these, after all, are mere externals. The dress is not the man. I speak, then, of higher matters. Touching the armies I should say, their officers are equal to ours,—I fear, take them all in all, they are *superior*. In strategy and masterly retreats, it is a clear case, that ours cannot begin with them in the former, or keep up with them, in the latter. But I wave all this. The contrast is not here.

What have been the moral developments, I ask, of this war? Where do we see humanity opening its gushing heart, amid scenes adapted to close it with strong bands of steel? and where has barbarism outstripped its former self in deeds of unwonted infamy? Go to the battle-field, and there read a lesson never to be forgotten. Where do you find, and upon whom do you charge the most fiendish cruelty? Who has assailed the wounded soldier, that lay bleeding and helpless on the ground, with thrust after thrust with the bayonet? Who dug up the body of a brave officer, and cut off his head, and burned his flesh to ashes? Who have stripped dead men of their apparel, and left them naked on the field to be eaten up of dogs, or to decay there? Who have crammed dungeons rank with filth and feculence with prisoners and the wounded, and denied the dying man a cup of cold water even, in the last extremity? Who have boiled the flesh from dead men's bones, and then manufactured these bones into ornaments for themselves and their friends, and for sale in the markets? Who have been in the habit of shooting their captives made in war, for showing their faces at the windows of their prison-house,—and then been elevated to special honors for such foul deeds? But I need not enlarge this truly humiliating catalogue. I ought

6

to add here, that this is not a fancy sketch, got up
for the occasion. I have drawn, not upon an
excited imagination, but upon sober facts, for this
dark picture. I have conned the details of recent
history, and not the wild romance of war, for what
I have now stated. These things, and much more
of the like character, is confirmed by credible
witnesses, and embodied in "the Report of the
joint Committee on the conduct of the present
war," made to the Senate of the United States, on
the 30th of April last. I subjoin a few details
from this document.

Mr. Nathaniel F. Parker, who was captured at
Falling Waters, Virginia, testifies, that the 'food of
the prisoners was always bad, and sometimes
nauseous; that the wounded had neither medical
attention, nor humane treatment, and that many
died from sheer neglect,—that five of the prisoners
were shot by the sentries outside, and that he saw
one man shot as he was passing his window on
the 8th of November, and that he died of his
wound on the 12th. The perpetrator of this foul
murder was subsequently promoted by the rebel
government.'

Dr. J. M. Homiston, surgeon of the Brooklyn
regiment, captured at Bull Run, testifies 'that when
he solicited permission to remain on the field to
attend to wounded men, some of whom were in a

helpless and painful condition and suffering for
water, he was brutally refused. They offered
him neither water nor any thing in the shape of
food. The secession surgeons would not allow
ours to perform operations on our own wounded,
but entrusted them to young assistants, some of
them with no *more knowledge of what they attempted
to do than an apothecary's clerk.'* The same witness
describes 'the sufferings of the wounded after the
battle as inconceivably horrible,—with bad food,
no covering, no water.' He adds—"Deaf to all
his appeals, they continued to refuse water to
the suffering men, and he was only enabled to
procure it by setting cups under the eaves to
catch the rain that was falling, and in this way
he spent the night, catching the water and convey-
ing it to the wounded to drink. The young surgeons seemed to delight in hacking and butcher-
ing the brave defenders of their country's flag,
while they were not permitted to operate upon
their own wounded."

William F. Swalm, assistant surgeon, testifies,
"that ten or twelve days after the battle (Bull
Run) he saw some of the Union soldiers unburied
on the field, and entirely naked. Walking around
were a great many women, gloating over the horrid
sight." The case of Dr. Ferguson, of one of the
New York regiments, is mentioned by Dr. Swalm.

"When getting into his own ambulance to look after his own wounded, he was fired upon by the rebels. When he told them who he was, they said they would take a parting shot at him, which they did, wounding him in the leg. He had his boots on, and his spurs on his boots, and as they drove along his spurs would catch in the tail board of the ambulance, causing him to shriek with agony. An officer rode up, and placing his pistol to his head, threatened to shoot him if he continued to scream. This was on Sunday, the day of the battle."

General James B. Ricketts, well known in Washington and throughout the country, after being wounded, in the battle of Bull Run, was captured; and "as he lay helpless on his back, a party of rebels passing by him cried out, *knock out his brains* the d—d Yankee." This brave officer was selected by the rebel authorities, when his condition was well known, as one of the hostages for the pirates. General Beauregard and General Winder to whom Gen. Ricketts was well known, were the two gentlemen—rather scoundrels—who made this selection. This witness confirms the statement, that "a number of our men were shot. In one instance two were shot; one was killed, and the other wounded, by a man who rested his gun on the window sill while he capped it. I heard of a great many of our prisoners who had been bayonetted and one of them shot. One was named Louis Francis, of the New York 14th. He had received fourteen bayonet-wounds—one of which was on the knee, in consequence of which his leg was amputated, after twelve weeks had passed. Dr. Peachy remarked to one of his young assistants, I wont be greedy; you may do it,—and he did it." But we have the whole case referred to by Gen. R., from Francis himself. He says, " I was attacked by two rebel soldiers, and wounded in the right knee with the bayonet. As I lay on the sod, they kept bayonetting me until I received fourteen wounds. One of them left me, the other remaining over me, when a Union soldier coming up, shot him in the breast, and he fell dead. I lay on the ground till 10 o'clock next day." Afterwards he was removed to Manassas and finally to Richmond. He adds, in his testimony, " My leg having partially mortified, I consented that it should be amputated, which operation was performed by a young man. The stitches and band slipped from neglect, and the bone protruded; and about two weeks after another operation was performed, at which time another piece of the thigh bone was sawed off." 'Six weeks after, and before the wound was healed, he was removed to the Tobacco Factory.' Two operations were subsequently performed on Francis—one at Fortress Monroe, and one at Brooklyn, after his release from captivity.

While General Ricketts was a prisoner and wounded, his wife came to visit him. He testifies, that "There were eight persons in the Lewis House, at Manassas, in the room where I lay; and my wife, for two weeks, slept in that room on the floor by my side, without a bed. When we got to Richmond there were six of us in a room, among them Col. Wilcox who remained with us until he was taken to Charleston. There we were all in one room. There was no door to it. The passage was filled with wounded soldiers; and in the hot summer months the stench from their wounds and the utensils they used, was fearful. There was no privacy at all, because there being no door, the room could not be closed. We were there as a common show." He adds, "General Johnson took my wife's carriage and horses at Manassas, kept them, and has them yet for ought I know. When I got to Richmond I spoke to several gentlemen about this, and so did Mrs. Ricketts. They said 'of *course* the carriage and horses should be returned.' They never were!" And, I may add here, 'of course,' they never will be.

The report adds, revolting as these disclosures are, it was when the committee came to examine witnesses in reference to the treatment of our heroic dead, that the fiendish spirit of the rebel leaders was most prominently exhibited. Daniel Bixby, Jr., of Washington, testifies,—'That he went out in company with Mr. G. A. Smart of Cambridge, Massachusetts, who went to search for the body of his brother, who fell at Blackburn Ford, in the action of the 18th of July. They found the grave. The clothes were identified.' "We found no head in the grave, and no bones of any kind—nothing but the clothes and portions of the flesh. We found the remains of three other bodies all together. The clothes were there; some flesh was left, but no bones." This witness also states, that Mrs. Pierce Butler, who lived near the place, said that she had seen the rebels boiling portions of the bodies of our dead in order to obtain their bones as relics. "She had seen drum-sticks made of *Yankee's bones*, as they called them." Mrs. Butler also stated " that she had seen a scull that one of the New Orleans Artillery had, which, he said, he was going to send home and have mounted, and that he intended to drink a brandy punch out of it the day he was married."

Frederick Scholes, of Brooklyn, testifies, among other things, as follows : " On Sunday morning I went out in search of my brother's grave. We found the trench, and dug for the bodies below. In one end of the trench we found, not more than two or three inches below the surface the thigh bone of a man which had evidently been dug up after the burial. While digging there a party of soldiers came along, and showed us a part of a shin bone, five or six inches long, which had the end sawed off. They said they had found it among other pieces in one of the cabins the rebels had deserted. From the appearance of it, pieces had been sawed off to make finger rings. As soon as the negroes noticed this, they said that the rebels had had rings made of the bones of the dead, and that they had them for sale in their camp."

The testimony of Gov. Sprague, of Rhode Island, confirms the statements, however revolting, of other witnesses. He visited the battle ground to search for the bodies of Col. Slocum and Major Ballou. 'He found that the body of Major Ballou had been mistaken for that of Col. Slocum, dug up, and the head cut off, and his body taken to a ravine, and there burned.' This was done by some Georgians who were greatly incensed against Col. Slocum, 'because he had destroyed about one half of their regiment, made up of their best citizens.' This was done says the Governor, "*in sheer brutality and nothing else.*" In searching for

Capt. Tower, the witness says, "in opening the ditch or trench, we found it filled with soldiers, all buried with their faces downward." And when asked 'whether he was satisfied that they were buried intentionally with their faces downward,'— his answer was: "Undoubtedly! Beyond all controversy."

But the other details I cannot give here. In the language of the Report, "The outrages upon the dead will revive the recollections of the cruelties to which savage tribes subject their prisoners. They were buried, in many cases, naked, with their faces downward; they were left to decay in the open air; their bones were carried off as trophies, sometimes, as the testimony proves. to be used as personal adornments, and one witness deliberately avers, that the head of one of our most gallant officers was cut off by a secessionist to be turned into a drinking cup on the occasion of his marriage. Monstrous as this revelation may appear to be, your committee have been informed. that during the last two weeks a scull of a Union soldier has been exhibited in the office of the Sergeant-at-Arms of the House of Representatives, which had been converted to such a a purpose, and which had been found on the person of, one of the rebel prisoners taken in a recent conflict. The testimony of Gov. Sprague of Rhode

7

Island, is most interesting. It confirms the worst reports against the rebel soldiers, and conclusively proves that the body of one of the bravest officers in the volunteer service, was burned. He does not hesitate to add that this hyena desecration of the honored corpse was because the rebels believed it to be the body of Col. Slocum, against whom they were infuriated for having displayed so much courage and chivalry in forcing his regiment fearlessly and bravely upon them."

I close these horrid details by saying, that no human institution in civilized life ever bred such men as form the basis and superstructure of this rebellion—*or could do it*—*except* SLAVERY. And yet many among us love it, and defend it. They look upon it as others do upon *rum*, as one of the great and good gifts of God. And too many who love the one, love the other also.

But this so called divine institution is doomed. It has all the sad marks of God's reprobation upon it. From its birth to its expiring hour, it is hardly greeted by a solitary ray of heaven's pure and blessed light. It begins in foreign rapine and plunder,—its cold blooded murders, during the middle passage, purple the Atlantic wave,—it was engrafted upon our system, at the close of the Revolution, in solemn mockery of all our national manifestoes, and in profane derision of the patriot-

blood that smoked upon our soil during our struggle for freedom and independence,—we have flat-
tered it by concessions, propped it up by compro-
mises, bribed it by special gratuities, defended its
life and honor by mob violence, made presidents
by the mysterious magic of its name, and told the
earth and the heavens of our determination to
cling to this American idol, if we cut loose from
every thing else. During the present fearful
struggle, the rebels have fought bravely to shield
it from injury and keep it from death, and we, by
many anomalous acts, have played the fool, for
the same purpose. Our generals in the field who
tried to make the traitor Breckenridge—*the slaveholders' candidate*—President, have been true to
their political instincts, and waged war *slowly*—
yea, TENDERLY, for fear of inflicting too severe a
punishment upon the rebels by marring their idol-
ized institution, and lest by overthrowing it alto-
gether, they might exterminate for ever the possi-
bility of all similar insurrections. The institution
must be spared as far as possible, and above all
its *tender roots* must be left unharmed in the soil.
Was ever national infatuation more absurd, or
more extravagant? Philosophy is the only true
expounder of history. *What* a man does, is a
simple fact,—*why* he does it, is the *rationale* of that
fact. But it will not all do. Slavery, in our

present agitations, is the all-pervading element. But the foundations of the system are breaking up. The proclamation of President Lincoln is doing its own work. Freedom to the captives, instead of being harmless as so much waste paper, or as the Pope's Bull against the comet, is a dagger in the heart of the rebellion. It was a bold step. I honor the man who could take it. It might well electrify and astonish two hemispheres. as it has done,—and leaving our world. which is deeply involved in the results, it is not too much to say, it may have electrified heaven and astonished hell. And when the year of Jubilee shall come, as come it will, and come it must—whether it be with the dawn of 1863. or at some later period— then this broad, goodly land, one—and indivisible for ever, shall celebrate the second *birth-day* of freedom. and the nations of the earth. and emancipated Africa among them, shall unite in one grand Anthem. and the earth and the heavens shall join in the universal chorus, as with "the voice of many waters. and the voice of mighty thunderings. saying, ALLALUIA: *for the Lord God omnipotent reigneth.*" Though *seventy-seven* years old to-day. I hope yet to live long enough to see these bright visions of the future fully accomplished.

AMEN.